MARIA'S many COLORS

Written by Breckyn Wood

Illustrated by Bojana Stojanovic

Cover design by Tina DeKam
© 2019 Jenny Phillips
www.goodandbeautiful.com

Chapter One

On a little brown town on top of a hill lived a girl named Maria. Maria's house was made of rough brown stones. The goats in her yard had coarse brown hair. Maria's dress was scratchy, patchy, and very, very brown.

Brown was not Maria's favorite color.

Six days of the week, Maria awoke with the sun. The yellow rays warmed her as she brushed her brown hair and put on her dress and sturdy brown shoes.

After her breakfast of brown bread and goat cheese, Maria went out into the yard to milk the goats, feed the brown chickens, and fill her basket with brown speckled eggs.

But on Sundays, Maria hopped out of bed before the

sun came peeking over the hills. Maria loved Sundays for one little reason and one big reason. The little reason was that on Sundays, Maria got

to wear a special dress. The fabric was pure white, but her mother had used every color of thread in her sewing basket to decorate the dress. Bright bunches of roses,

bluebells, daisies, and lilies grew up the front and along the collar, their green leaves twisting together. Scarlet parrots and golden finches soared on the sleeves.

Maria loved that dress, and she loved her mother for the many days and nights she had spent bent over the dress, her silver needle flashing in the light.

The big reason Maria loved Sundays was that Sundays meant church, and church meant songs and prayers and friends and colors—so many wonderful colors. The windows in the church were stained glass, which means they were like beautiful paintings. When the sun shined directly through one of the windows, the whole church was filled with heavenly light.

Chapter Two

One night as Maria lay snug in her bed, a terrible storm blew through her town. The rain pounded like drums on the roof. The wind howled and made tree branches screech and scrape against the side of her house. The thunder boomed. The lightning split the sky down the middle.

But Maria was not sad or

afraid, because tomorrow
was Sunday. With that happy
thought, Maria snuggled down
in her cozy brown blanket
and went back to sleep.

When Maria and her family got to church the next morning, a sad sight met their eyes. "Oh, no!" Maria cried.

"How awful," her mother said.

"Yes, what a shame," her father agreed, shaking his head.

"Wow," her two big brothers said, their eyes and mouths open wide.

Soon other people had gathered around. Everyone

was looking up at the church, where two of the beautiful windows had been smashed to pieces. A big old tree, pushed over by the night's storm, was still leaning against the side of the building.

Chapter Three

$\mathcal{E}$verybody in the village spent that Sunday morning clearing away branches from the churchyard and sweeping up the broken

glass. When Maria saw those wonderful blues, greens, and reds being thrown in the trash, she felt a lump rise in her throat. When she looked at the big open holes where the two windows used to be, tears pricked at her eyes.

After the villagers had cleaned as best as they could, Maria's pastor climbed the church steps and spoke to the crowd.

"Thank you, my friends, for your hard work this day. Some of our windows may be gone, but I thank the Lord that we have all been kept safe from the storm. May He bless us and watch over us as we return to our homes." He then lifted a large jar and showed it to the crowd. "We will be collecting money to replace the windows. I know many of you cannot give much, but I hope we will all give what we can."

As everyone turned to leave, Maria tugged at her mother's hand. "Mama, will the windows be fixed soon? Will there be new ones when we come back next week?"

Her mother's eyes looked sad. "No, sweetheart, I don't think so. It will cost a lot of money to get new windows, and we are not a rich town—"

A loud *bang, bang, bang* made her stop talking. She

and Maria looked back at the church and saw two men hammering pieces of wood over the empty window frames. They looked like bandages over the poor broken church.

As Maria slowly walked back home, the banging of the hammers matched the banging of her heart. She didn't know how, but she was going to find a way to help fill that jar.

Chapter Four

The problem of how to help fix the church pounded in Maria's head all the next day.

"If only the chickens would lay twice as many eggs," she thought as she put the speckled eggs in her basket—just enough to feed her and her family.

"If only the goats would make twice as much milk," she thought as the warm white stuff sloshed into her blue bucket—just enough for her and her family to drink and make a little cheese.

Only when she went for her
afternoon walk up in the hills
did Maria find her answer. It
was springtime, and when

she reached the top of the
first hill, she saw spread out
before her thousands and
thousands of wildflowers.
They danced happily in the
breeze, waving to her and
sending her their sweet smell.

This was it! She would
gather them by the bunches
and sell them at the market.

Maria dropped to her
knees and began filling the
brown skirt of her dress with
blossoms of pink, purple,
red, and yellow.

Chapter Five

Maria woke up even earlier now. She got dressed in the dark, ate breakfast in the dark, and did her chores by the light of the stars and moon. In that dim light, everything looked the same—gray all around. But by the time Maria reached the top of her hill, the sun would start to fill the sky with deep red and rich gold. Its rays shined on the rainbow of flowers in the grass.

Her water buckets and hands filled with as many bunches as she could carry, Maria started on the long walk to the market.

People from the hills and
towns all around came to the
village square to sell the food
from their farms and things
they made. Maria loved to
see the fresh, juicy fruits, the
smooth clay pots, and the

carved wooden animals of
every shape and size.

   Maria did not have a table
to sell from, but a friendly
old lady let Maria share
her space. The woman sold
dresses decorated all over

with colorful thread, like
Maria's special Sunday dress.

"How do you have so
many?" Maria asked in
wonder after the first day at
the market. "It took my mama
many months to make just
one for me."

The woman smiled, giving
her kind face even more
wrinkles. "Your mama has
many other things to do,"
she said. "She must take care
of the house and cook and
clean and teach you and your

brothers. I am old and my children are all grown up. They take care of me now, so I can spend most of each day at my needle."

Maria and the old lady chatted as people walked back and forth in the market. Some of them stopped to look at the flowers, some at the dresses. Some didn't stop at all. As they talked and waited, the woman kept at her needle and Maria arranged her flowers into

pretty bunches—big ones
to fill clay pots and small
ones for ladies to pin to their
dresses.

When the market closed
each day, Maria would walk
past the church to visit the
pastor before going home
and put her few coins in
the collection jar. He always
thanked her kindly, but
Maria could see that the jar
was not filling up very fast.
When she said this to the

pastor, he sighed. "I know, my dear. But people have many other things to worry about—growing their crops and feeding their families. I guess these old windows will have to wait a long time."

Chapter Six

One morning as Maria sat at the market braiding some flowers into a crown, she heard in the distance a sound she had only heard a few times before in her village—the *vroom vroom* of a car.

Everyone in the market looked up and stared. This was no farm truck, rusted

and squeaky with age. It
was the shiniest thing Maria
had ever seen, like sunlight
bouncing off water, and as
red as a summer tomato.

A man hopped out of the
car and closed the door with

a bang. The sun was baking the brown stones of the square, but he looked cool and clean in his crisp, white clothes.

The villagers all began talking at once, holding their

items out to the rich man
and inviting him to come to
their booths.

"Melons, sir, sweet and ripe!"

"A new leather belt for you,
sir? Handmade, very good
price!"

"Hand-painted clay pots, one of a kind, sir!"

The man smiled kindly at the people who showed him their goods, but he didn't stop until he reached Maria's booth. His eyes lit up as he looked at the colorful dresses.

"My wife would love one of these," he said. "You do amazing work, señora."

The old lady looked pleased. "Thank you, señor. I

do what I can with the hands God gave me."

"Well, I can see He has blessed them. I will take this dress for my wife," he said, picking one covered in roses of red, yellow, and pink, "and I would like one for my daughter as well. She is always sad when she can't travel with me." He turned his bright smile on Maria. "She is just about your size. How old are you?"

"I am almost ten, sir."

"My girl is almost nine, and she loves flowers." He looked at Maria's colorful display. "I wish I could bring her some of these, but I don't think they would last

on the long trip home."

Maria looked sad at these words, so he said quickly, "But I will take these two big bunches for my sisters. I am driving to visit them this afternoon. And I will take

this one," he said, picking up a stalk of bluebells from her water bucket, "for me." And he put it in the front pocket of his shirt, where it added a happy splash of blue to the white.

"Thank you!" Maria cried as she added the jingling coins to her small pile.

"So, señora, do you have a dress that would fit my girl?" he asked, turning back to the old woman.

The woman frowned. "I am sorry, but the only dress I have of that size is at home. It will not be finished for weeks."

The man's smile dimmed. "That is too bad. I am going home in a few days. Is there no way it could be finished by then? I would be willing to pay extra, of course." And he named a sum of money that made Maria gasp.

"Not for twice so much could I finish it in time, I

am afraid," the woman said
sadly. "I am sorry."

The man paid her well for
the rose dress and turned,
with flowers in each hand,
back to his car. Just as he
sat in the driver's seat,
ready to pull away, Maria
came gasping up to him, her
brown sandals kicking up
the dust.

"Hello again!" he said.

"Sir," Maria said, taking
big breaths and trying not
to cough. She wanted to

say this quickly, before she changed her mind. "Sir, I . . . I have a dress. My mother made it for me, but I will sell it to you for your daughter. It is even more beautiful than the dress for your wife." And Maria told the man about the church windows and the storm.

"I wondered what had happened when I drove past," he said. "Your church does indeed have some lovely stained glass."

"Can you come back
tomorrow morning? I will
have the dress ready for you
then."

The man agreed to come
back. He waved to Maria as
he drove down the road and
out of sight.

Chapter Seven

When Maria got home, she went to the clothes line. Her family's clothes were dancing in the breeze, her Sunday dress the one bright spot among all the browns.

Maria pulled the dress down gently and wrapped it in brown paper. She wiped a few tears from her eyes

and then went to pick more flowers for the market.

The next morning, Maria sat at the booth clutching the package in her lap. She jumped every time she heard a loud sound, thinking it was the rich man's car.

"Don't worry, child," said the old woman. "He promised to come, so he will come."

Soon, the tomato-red car drove up again, and the rich man walked through the market to their booth.

"I believe you have something for me?" he said to Maria with a smile.

Maria handed him the package and tried her best to smile too. The man pulled back the paper to peek at the dress. For a few moments, he didn't say anything. Maria was worried. Maybe he didn't like her mother's work as much as the old lady's! Then he spoke.

"I'm afraid I can't pay you the amount I said yesterday for this dress," he said.

Maria's heart pounded.

"It is even more beautiful than I hoped. You must let me pay more." And he pulled

from his pocket a small
brown bag that was heavy
with coins. Maria stared at
it, not knowing what to say.

"Thank you, señor," the old
woman spoke for her. "That
is very generous."

"No more than it is worth,
I'm sure," he said, looking
into Maria's eyes. "I will
make sure my daughter
treasures it."

The story of Maria's dress
spread quickly through

the market. After the man had driven away, people crowded around her booth. Everyone suddenly wanted flowers for their tables, for their mothers, for their hair. For the first time ever, Maria sold all of her flowers before the market closed.

That day when she went to visit the pastor with her big bag of coins, there was a long line in front of the church doors. People were

talking excitedly, and when they saw Maria, they pushed her to the front of the line. When Maria saw the collection jar on the pastor's desk, she couldn't believe it. It was more than halfway full! The pastor smiled at her, and everyone laughed with joy as they heard the ringing clink, clink, clink of Maria's many coins raining into the jar.

Chapter Eight

A few months later, Maria sat in church with her family. She wore her scratchy brown dress now, but that was okay. She sang loudly and happily, and every time she looked up at the two shiny, new, colorful windows, her heart soared.

The pastor stood up and began to read: "Consider the lilies, how they grow . . ."

As she listened, Maria looked out over all the people in the church and noticed something she hadn't noticed before—flowers. They were her flowers, the pinks, yellows, purples, and reds. They were pinned to women's dresses, sticking out of men's front pockets, and crowning the dark braids of little girls. Her booth had been very busy since the day she sold her dress.

Saying goodbye to her beautiful, colorful dress had been so hard, but as the sun shined through the

stained glass windows and

everyone stood to sing

another song, Maria realized

she had helped bring color to her little brown town in more ways than one.

The End

Try a Level 3* Book from
The Good and the Beautiful Library

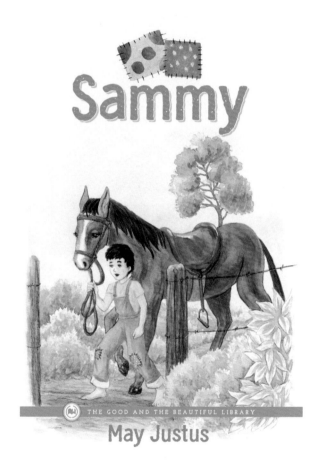

Sammy

THE GOOD AND THE BEAUTIFUL LIBRARY

May Justus

*Reading level assessment is available on
www.goodandbeautiful.com*